The adventures of the magical suitcase

Anita Darlene Ice

I

II

Dedication:

This book is dedicated to every child I had the blessing to teach in some capacity, may you always be true to yourself. To the magic that is reading, that takes us to places in the world we've never been but always wanted to go to experience new people and cultures. Thank you to my friends and my circle Chloe, Natalie, Nancy, Michelle and Shaun for continuous love and support...

Oh, the places I have seen!! Hello, my name is Lucy! I am soft-sided, rectangular, and 45'x75 inches tall. Some of the handy features are four rolling wheels and lots of storage pockets. My skin is blue in color with flowers. I can be used flat or upright, and wow, look at me go just with a pull!!

Did you know I can be filled to your heart's content? But, please do not sit on my body. My owner has a habit of filling me with shoes, clothes, and even scuba stuff. Then she sat on me, well, that flipper went flying out, and no more scuba gear in my belly.

Oh, the places I have had to go...
The airport is my least favorite place. The airport baggage handlers have a hard job, but they toss me here or there and everywhere. I am so grateful I don't have stickers on my body. I have enjoyed meeting friends from all over the world n the cold cargo bags as we travel to exotic places.

6

I remember when I really was my owner's best frien
We travelled fearlessly around the globe and saw so
people, places, and exciting things. I think Hawaii an
Japan were some of my favorite places.

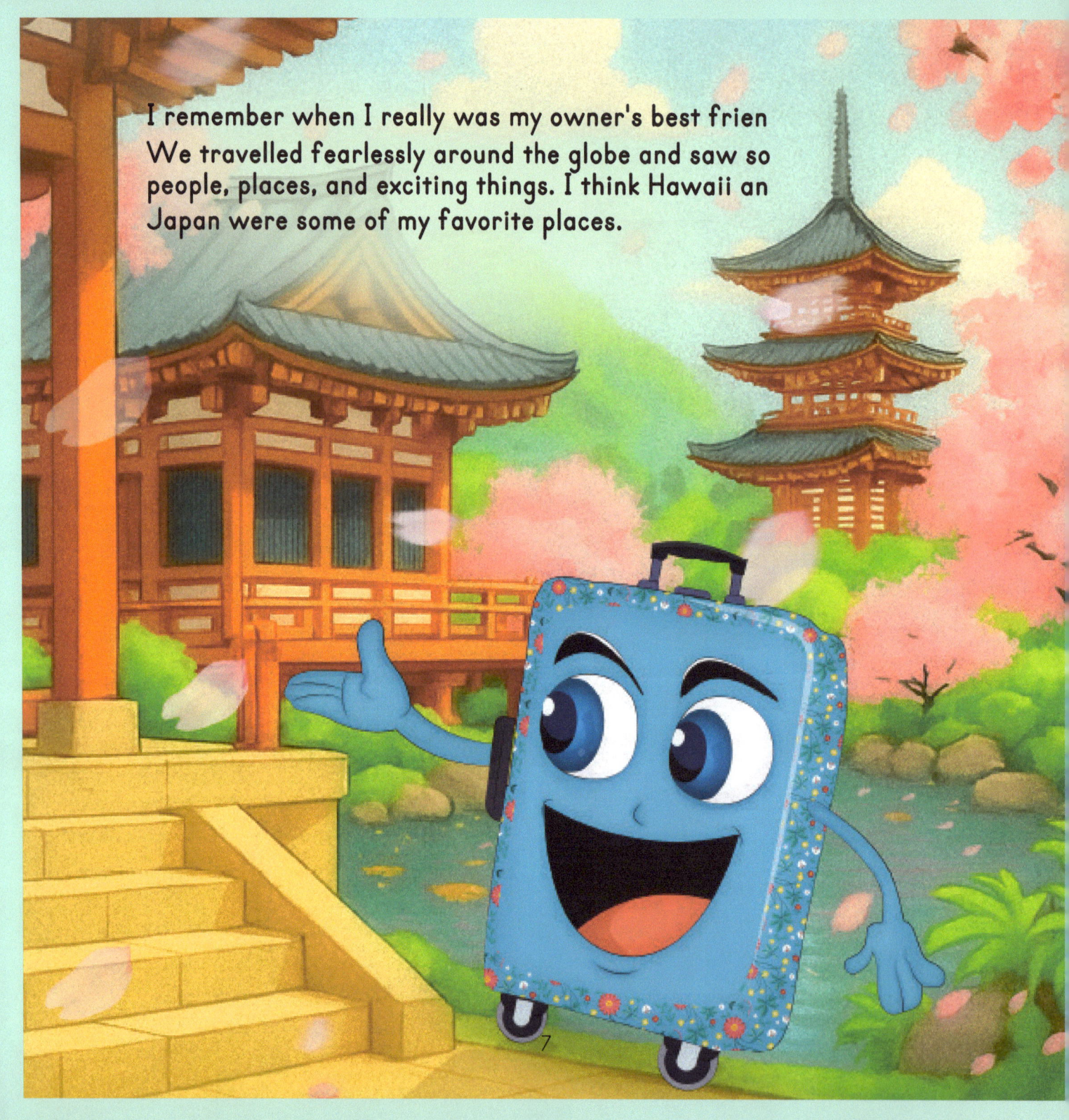

7

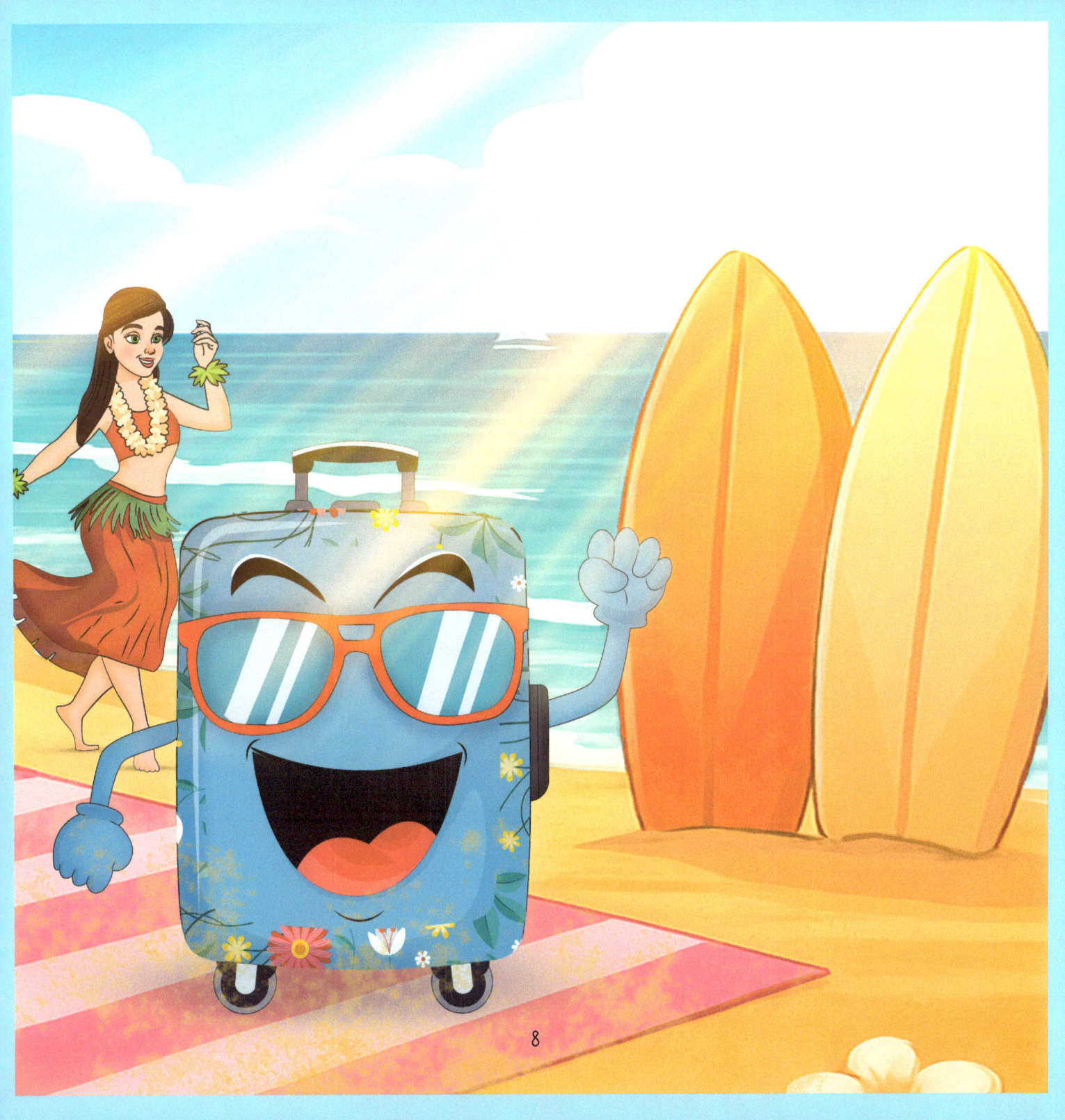

8

Sometimes I would be separated from my owner when I missed the connection and had to wait until another flight left so I could catch up.
I always made friends wherever I would go!!

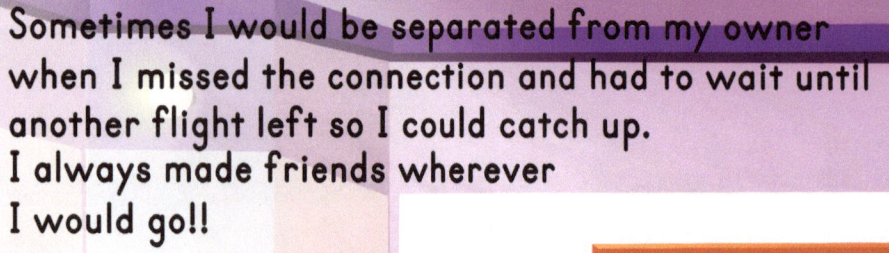

10

Another one of my favorite places was Holland, where my owner lived as a small girl. The airport was so clean, and I especially enjoyed the visits to see the windmills, markets, and flower gardens.

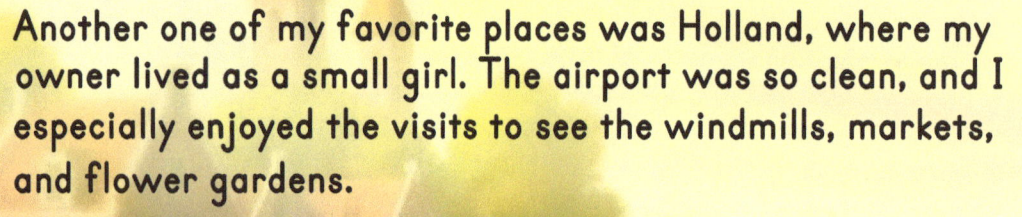

12

One of my most unique places was the Monteverde Cloud Forest in Costa Rica. There I was in the middle of a rainforest with the moist, hot, wet weather in a tent...with a 7-foot iguana resting on me for a nap!!

13

14

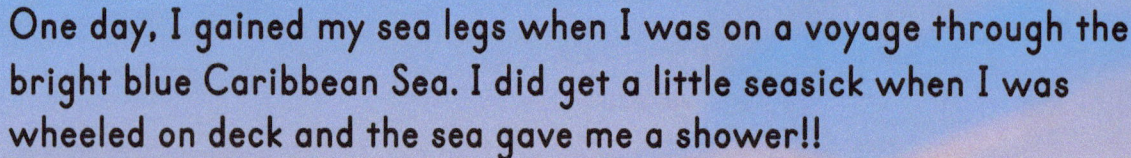

One day, I gained my sea legs when I was on a voyage through the bright blue Caribbean Sea. I did get a little seasick when I was wheeled on deck and the sea gave me a shower!!

Another favorite trip was when we learning how to sail and surf in the Grenadines. It was kind of tight quarters, and my friends were lifejackets. But the waves lulled me to sleep, and I watched through the porthole.

I don't always follow my owner's directions, but it's not really my fault. There have been times when I should have been in Japan and ended up in Germany in a strange airport. My owner must have been sad because I have a responsibility to carry her worldly belongings. I do feel sad when I am separated from her.

19

Over the last few years, I have not been traveling as I had in the past due to a change of careers and a dedication to children. My new home is a closet, and sometimes boxes fall on my head, and I feel sad just waiting here to go on my next adventure.

21

22

I have wonderful memories of visiting Hawaii, Japan, Holland, Costa Rica, Barbados, and the beautiful Caribbean islands.

23

24

I am proud to announce that it is my 15th birthday, and I am still in excellent shape!! I am thankful for my adventures and all the friends I have met.

25

Wow, I turned 16 and look at my new wheels, and I am off on my next adventure around the world!!

Japan

North America

Grenadines

Hawaii

Costa Rica

South America

Europe

Amsterdam

Asia

Africa

Australia

Antarctica